THE

POWER

OF

YOUR

IMAGINATION

A CREATIVE COLORING AND JOURNALING BOOK WITH POSITIVE QUOTES.

SANDY STOTLER

DEDICATION

To my mom, you are the wind beneath my wings. Love you always.

For my daughters who both have occupations in the field

of helping others, I am so proud of you both

And I love you.

"JUST WHEN THE CATERPILLAR THOUGHT THE WORLD WAS OVER, IT BECAME A BUTTERFLY"

-Chuang Tzu

<u>Are you a caterpillar or a butterfly and why?</u>

"Uniqueness
Is what makes
You
The most
Beautiful"

- Lea Michele

What makes you unique?

_____

_____

_____

_____

_____

_____

_____

_____

_____

_____

_____

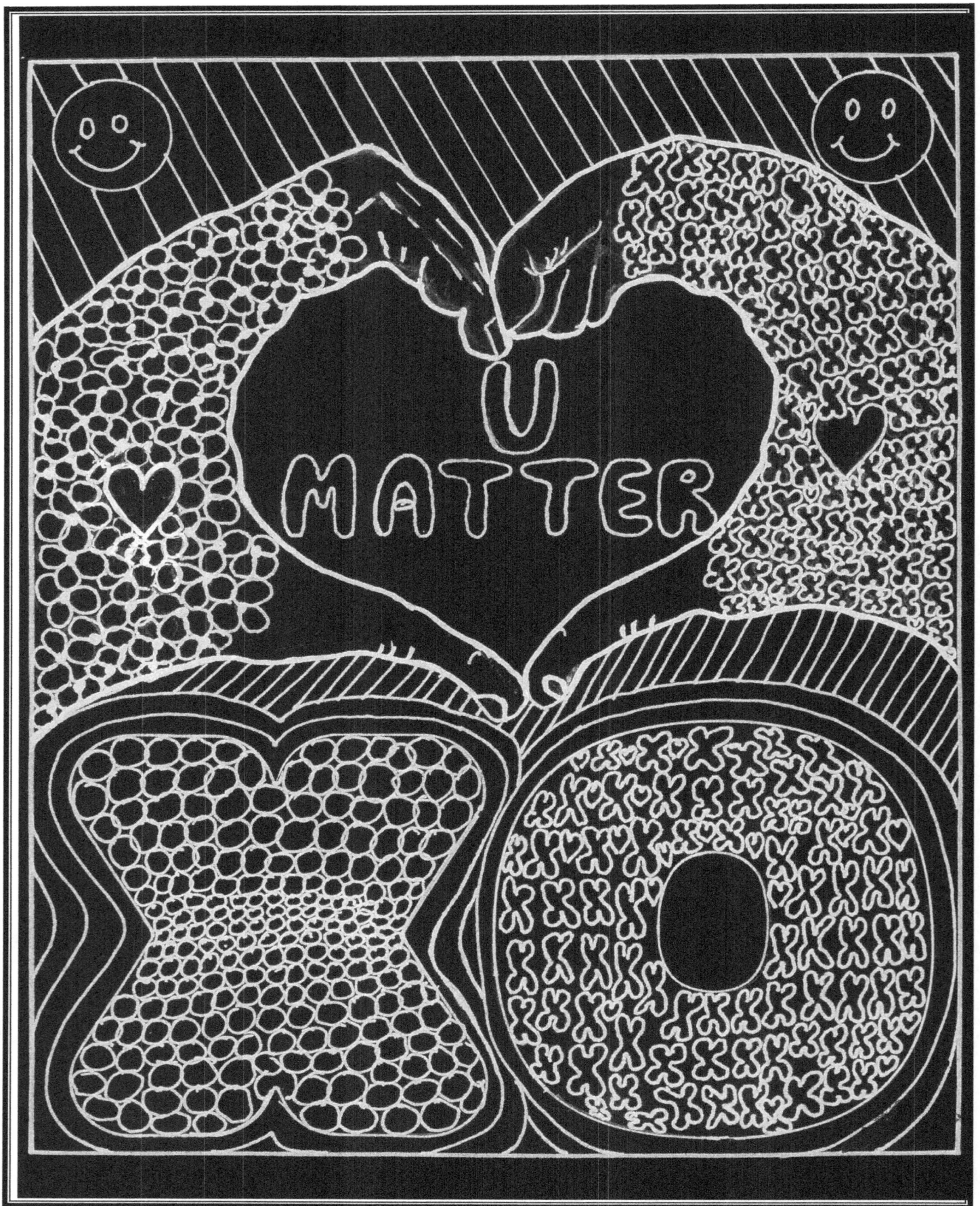

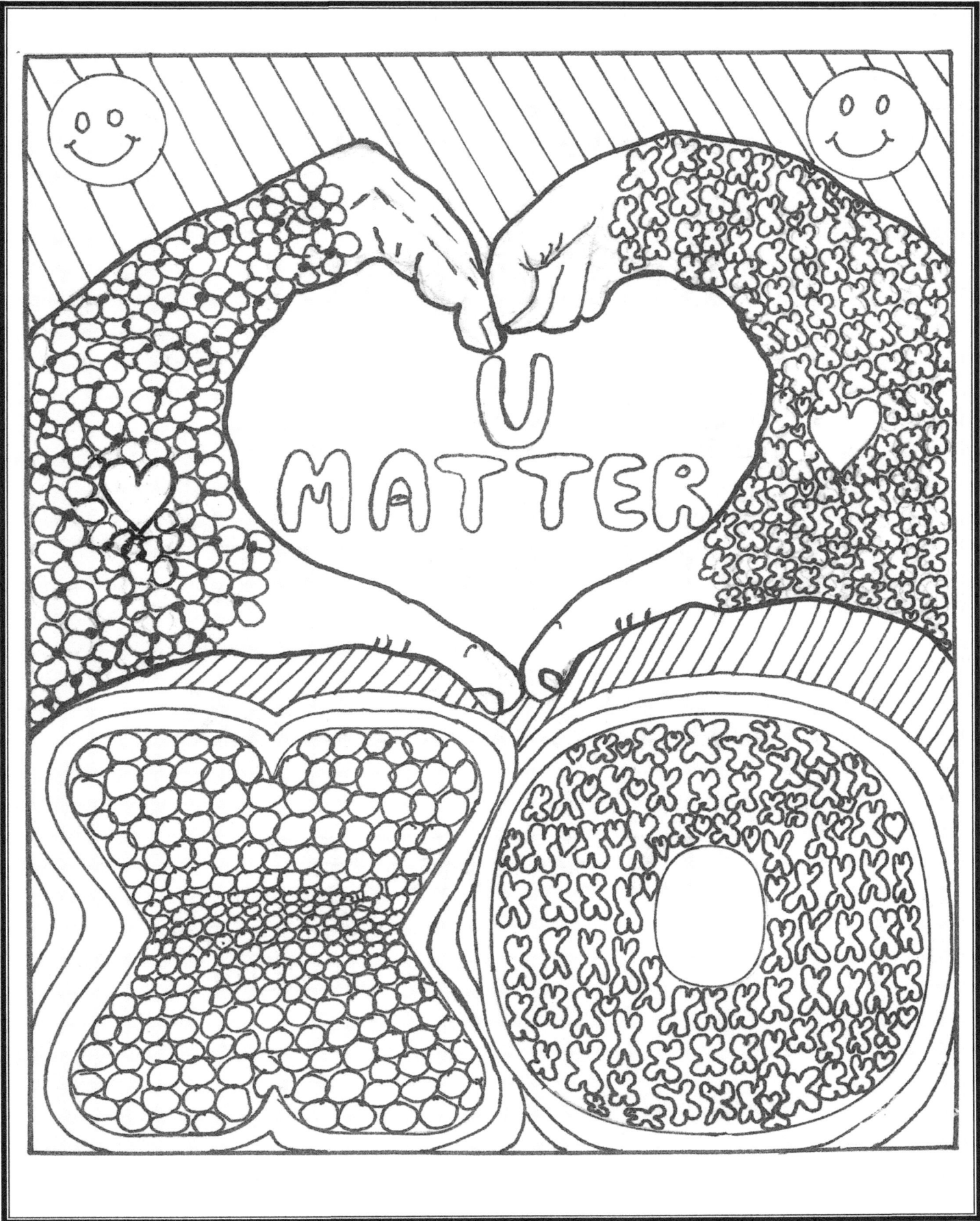

YOU ARE
NOT A DROP
IN THE OCEAN.
YOU ARE THE
ENTIRE OCEAN
IN A DROP"

-Rumi

What matters to you?

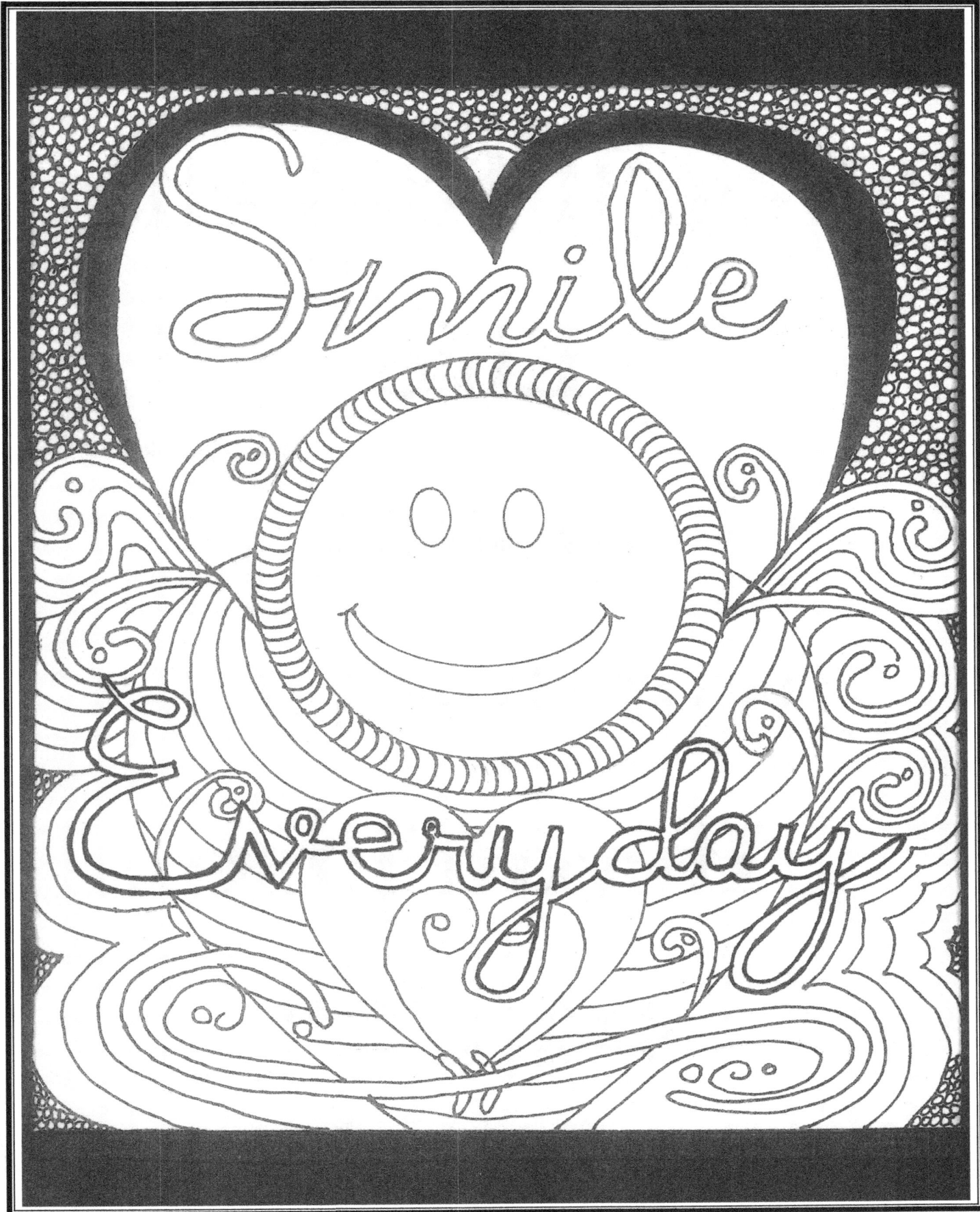

"You'll find that
Life
Is still
worthwhile,
If you just
SMILE."

-Charles Chaplin

What makes you smile?

_____

_____

_____

_____

_____

_____

_____

_____

_____

_____

_____

#6 "If I am happy inside,

Then I live in

Paradise

No matter where

My residence

Is."

-Mac Anderson

What or where is paradise to you?

"Imagine All the People Living life in Peace."

-John Lennon

How do you imagine peace for you?

"Music gives a soul

To the universe,

Wings to the mind,

Flight

To the imagination

And life to everything."

- Plato

What kind of music does you like and why?

_____

_____

_____

_____

_____

_____

_____

_____

_____

_____

A flower does not

Think of competing

With the flower

Next to it,

It just blooms."

- Zen Shin

What does this quote mean to you?

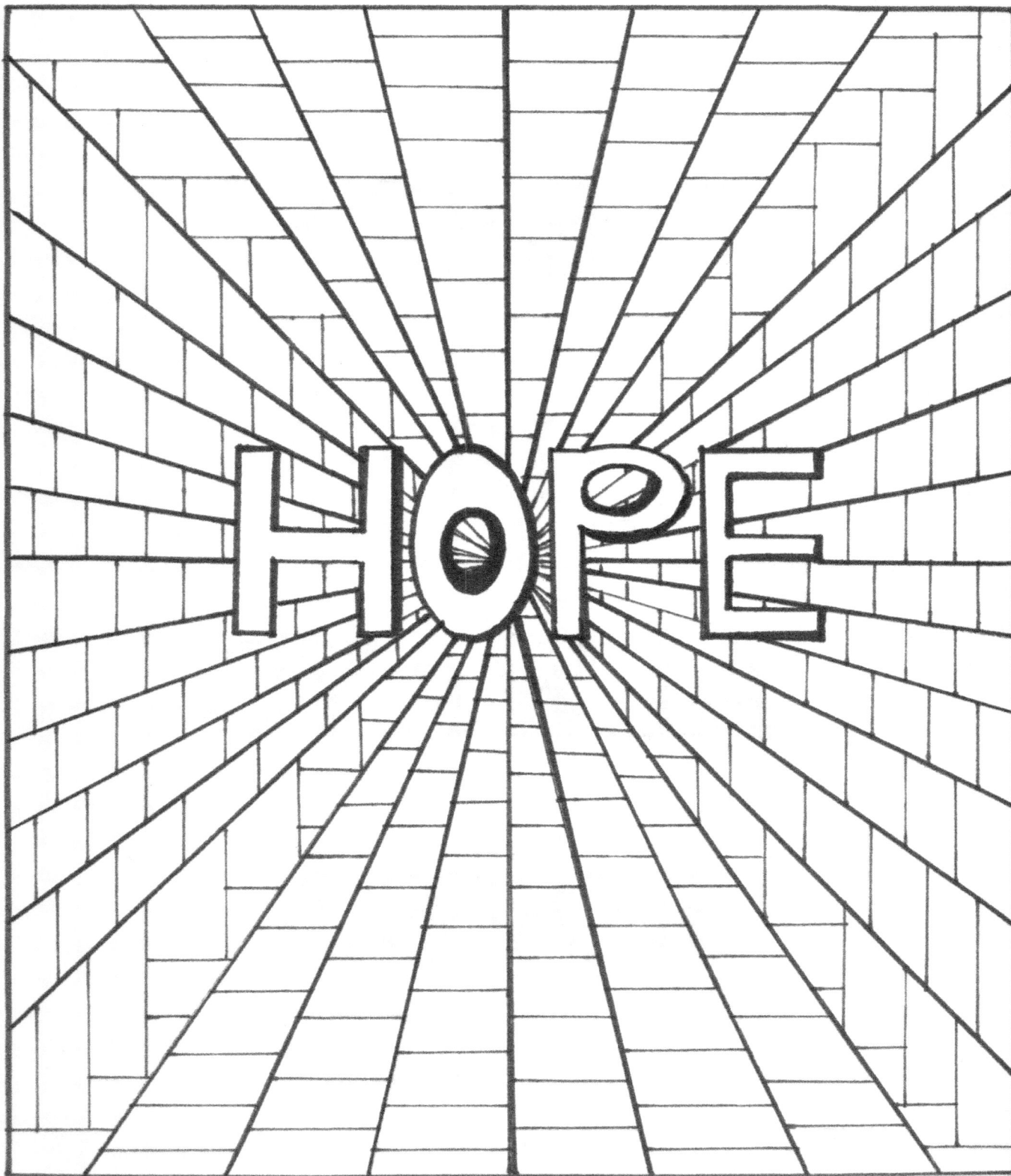

"THERE

IS

ALWAYS

HOPE."

-Unknown

What do you hope for?

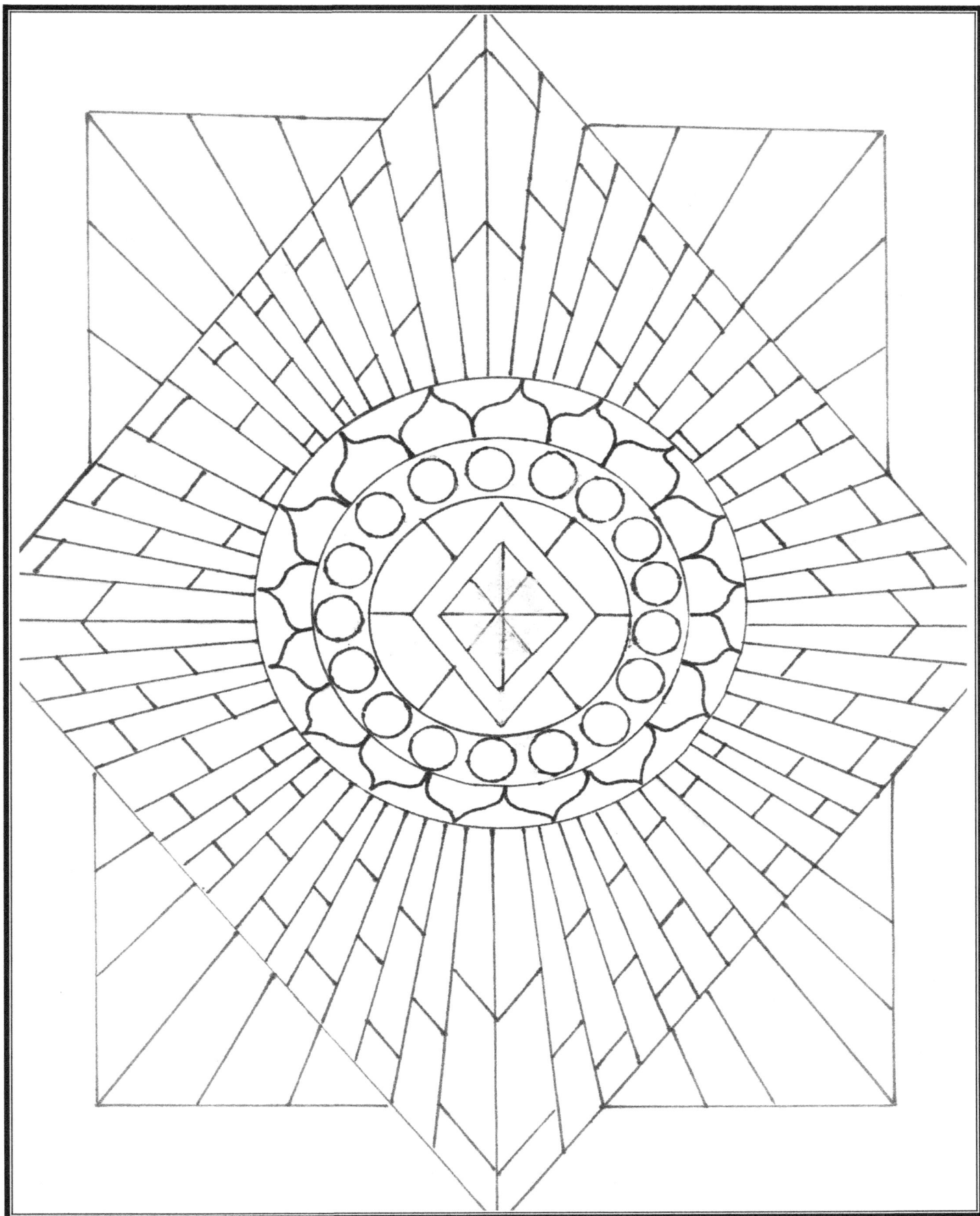

"In a gentle way,

You can shake

The world."

-Mahatma Gandhi

In a gentle way, how can you make a difference?

_____

_____

_____

_____

_____

_____

_____

_____

_____

_____

_____

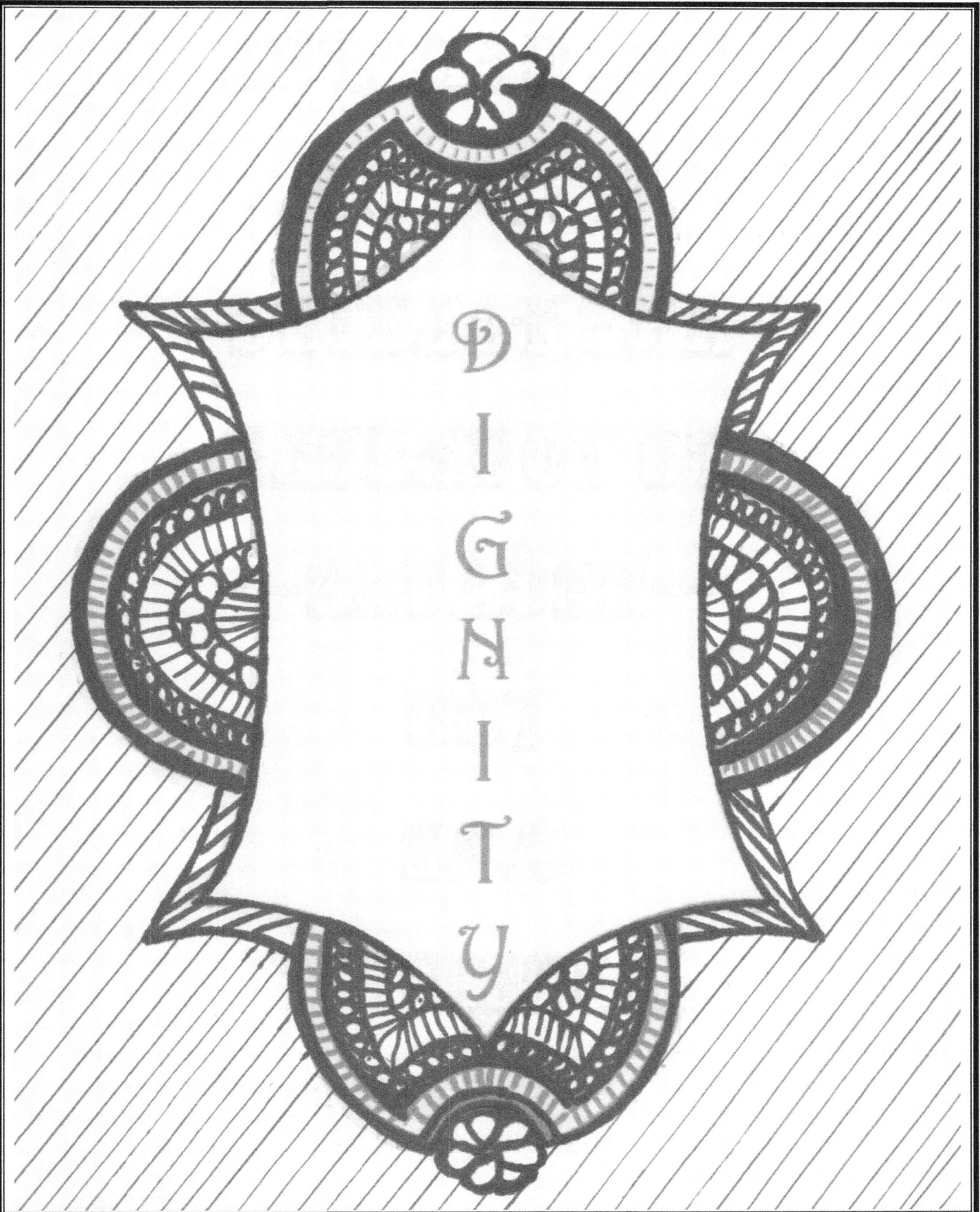

DIGNITY

" BE CAREFUL HOW YOU ARE TALKING TO YOURSELF ---BECAUSE--- YOU ARE LISTENING"

-Lisa M. Hayes

What do you say to yourself and how can you improve that conversation?

"Sunflowers
End up facing
The sun,
But they go
Through a lot of dirt
To find their way
there."

-J.R. Rim

How are you taking care of yourself?

_____

_____

_____

_____

_____

_____

_____

_____

_____

_____

_____

_____

_____

_____

Yesterday

Is History

Tomorrow

Is a Mystery

Today

Is a Gift...?

That's why they call

It present"

-Master Oogway

<u>What positive things can you do today?</u>

Suggestions of positive things to do today:

Call a relative or friend

Go for a walk

Hug your pet

Listen to music

Take long slow breathes in and out

Color in a coloring book

Smile

Add positive things you can do in 30 minutes or less:

_____

_____

_____

_____

ADDITIONAL PAGES FOR JOURNALING OR DRAWING

ABOUT THE AUTHOR

Sandy Stotler is the author and illustrator of THE POWER OF YOUR IMAGINATION. She has two daughters, five grandchildren. Ms. Stotler resides in California. She loves to draw and write. She hopes this "self-help book" can provide support to anyone who is reaching out for a positive experience.

You are invited to write to Sandy at: writer4you@live.com with positive questions or suggestions for her next book to help others.

Made in the USA
Las Vegas, NV
17 January 2025